Ghosts mark the passage of time in their own way.

"It's all in pretty good shape down here," Amy said. "Maybe that luck will hold with the rest of the house."

Missy glanced back over her shoulder, eyes narrowed a bit but not giving a thing away. She led the way up the stairs and through the open trapdoor and into the darkness above.

When Amy stepped up onto the lovely old hardwood floor, she scowled at a curving set of deep gouges in the wide boards. She started to stay something to Missy, but stopped cold at the look on her face.

Missy's full lips were compressed, and her eyebrows drawn down toward her dark blue eyes. She didn't look angry, though, like Amy had just been.

Missy looked afraid.

"What did—" Amy started, then her gaze followed Missy's.

She breathed in a sharp gasp of the thick, musty air.

Gouges weren't the only thing marking the floor.

Walking the Ghosts: A Voices through Time Novella

Published 2019 by Spiral Publishing, Ltd.
www.spiralpublishing.net
St. Paul, Virginia

ISBN-13: 978-1-948890-28-1
Large Print ISBN-13: 978-1-948890-30-4

LOC NUMBER: 2019950309

To Kevin

For everything.

And for asking me what was next after reading Songs in the Mountain. As is often the case, you knew me better than I did.

WALKING THE GHOSTS

A VOICES THROUGH TIME NOVELLA

KARI KILGORE

SPIRAL PUBLISHING, LTD.

Chapter 1

THE LAST THING Amy Johnstone had ever expected to be was a homeowner. Nineteen years as a dedicated renter up in Chicago suited her just fine, thank you very much. Someone else to do the maintenance, no lawn to mow, neighbors as anonymous as she was.

And yet here she sat, huddled in a tiny rental car, clutching her stomach and a set of house keys the extremely friendly lawyer back in town said belonged to her. Trying her best not to either hyperventilate or throw up.

Staring up at the old Johnstone home place that she hadn't seen for the last thirty years.

Well, as close as she could get to staring, with the way the long, curving driveway twisted through towering maples, poplars, oaks, and vast piles of overgrown grass and brush. Amy couldn't actually see much more than a peek of gray stone, a glimpse of shingled roof.

The constant wind up along Abrams Ridge kept shifting that view as it carried the gentle kiss of rich, summertime growth in the Blue Ridge Mountains. If her memory of smells hadn't failed with all those years of city living, no one had kept the honeysuckle growing along the edge of the sprawling front yard trimmed back.

Her Great Auntie Maybelle had loved that honeysuckle, even when it threatened to overgrow down into the garden plot generations of Johnstones had survived on, during good times or bad. Amy's early-morning-and-airline-food upset stomach still managed to grumble at the memory of the sweetest corn she'd ever tasted dripping with rich butter from the family cow.

She managed to sit back and turn her head, searching for traces of the barn trapped in a thick, green mat of gigantic kudzu leaves. If it was still there, the rambling structure's days of sheltering a cow, a few chickens, and an occasional horse were long past. The lightning-fast growth of kudzu was merciless on old wooden buildings once it got started.

Amy jingled the keys in her hand, wondering why there were so many when the barn was clearly a lost cause. A bunch of them, either silver or brass, every one scarred and scratched enough to be as old as she was at forty-one.

The past several months of adjusting to working from home—and the very likely related slow-motion breakup of a five-year relationship—created enough dings and dents to make her feel a hell of a lot closer to fifty.

She took a deep breath, realized inhaling the chemical aroma of freshly deodorized and cleaner-sprayed rental car was a mistake, and stepped out onto the weedy driveway. No one would be driving any kind of sedan up here until a mower or maybe a tractor cleared the way.

She'd barely made it half a mile off the beaten up and badly in need of repair slab of pavement that passed for a main road.

Looked like no one had driven along the driveway in *any* kind of vehicle for at least ten years.

Her worn out and decidedly out-of-fashion blue jeans

had definitely been a good idea, even for meeting Art Steffens, an attorney she'd never heard of before last week. Thankfully his own clothes and decidedly odd office décor had been almost as casual.

He'd tried his best, but Amy had been too tired and stunned to take in much of his explanations of who died when, the end of this lawsuit and the other, and how that all led to her owning the house and a few hundred acres of land. His attempts to explain why the town had even managed to change *names* in her long absence. From Hartstown to Bountyfield, Virginia.

Just one more thing to keep her off-balance.

The weedy mess she was about to walk through reached past her knees, so nice pants—or even worse, a skirt—would have been a nightmare.

The same accidental forethought held true with wrangling her long auburn hair into a fairly stable knot at the base of her neck. All the better to avoid the branches and vines that arched down from overhead.

Amy wasn't sure what the tall, spindly weeds with spiked seed heads on the top were, or the spongy yellowish ground cover. She strongly suspected the three-leafed vine snaking through it was poison ivy, something she hadn't missed for even one second of her time away from here.

At least the weather was cooperating for the moment. The sky was clear blue with scattered rafts of fluffy clouds, and the breeze kept it far cooler than July in Chicago. Of course back in Chicago Amy could actually *see* the sky. The whole sky, and miles and miles of it above the grid of the city and the endless waves of Lake Michigan.

Here she felt hemmed in even before she stepped into the green overgrowth tunnel, surrounded by tree-covered mountains jutting up all around even at what had to be a couple of thousand feet above her normal elevation. She had the uncomfortable pressure in her ears and slight lightheadedness to prove it.

She didn't remember feeling so closed off and isolated here as a little girl. Paradise had given way to paranoia.

She resisted the urge to lock the car and started walking toward the house.

Her house, as of three o'clock that afternoon.

Amy jumped like a spooked cat at a rustling disturbance somewhere to her left. Determined to keep her cool for any ghosts that could possibly be watching, she slowly turned that way.

Two huge gray squirrels chased each other through last autumn's crispy dry leaves, then ran halfway up a big oak tree. They stopped, gripping the ridged bark in a wide-legged stance, facing each other with one upside down.

Amy laughed out loud when both lifted their shining black eyes to stare at her. She slipped her iPhone out of her pocket for a picture and wasn't surprised to see not a trace of cellular signal.

"That obvious, huh? That I haven't been here since the Eighties?" Both squirrels streaked out of sight toward the top of the tree before she could open the camera app, chattering at her for even trying.

"Thanks for the welcome. I'll show myself around."

She kept walking, wishing she'd packed a pair of boots instead of low-top walking shoes. Trying to navigate the ancient gravel road when she couldn't see where the ruts and rocks were through the weeds was doing a number on her ankles.

How much would it cost to get this old driveway mowed, much less repaired or re-graveled or whatever people who lived several miles away from the last road with lines on it did when the potholes got too big? She was pretty sure the big city solution of slapping a metal plate down to cover the worst of it between repaving jobs wouldn't work out here.

Amy jumped again and actually let out a little shriek when three huge black birds took off from a gnarled old apple tree in the biggest curve in the driveway.

Crows, that's all.

A series of harsh answering *caws* reassured her, at least a little.

She and her cousins and neighbor kids had tormented and teased each other how the vultures would circle overhead if they got separated and lost out in these woods, but by then it would be too late. They'd be trapped, getting body parts plucked away like the eagle devouring Prometheus's liver over and over again. Quite the imaginations they'd had back then, like any herd of free-roaming children tended to before the days of play dates and overscheduled summer vacations.

Amy wondered for probably the hundredth time since she left Mr. Steffens's office back in Bountyfield, house keys in hand, why none of that herd of cousins had ended up with the old Johnstone home place. She hoped the whispers in her mind—that they all lived close by or visited more often so they knew something she didn't—were simply more evidence of her paranoia.

Turning the next corner and finally getting a full view of the house didn't do a damn thing to calm that particular anxiety, or any of the others racing through Amy's mind.

She could make out the gradual rise of the broad, sweeping lawn only because several patches of tall weeds had been knocked flat. Probably by last winter's snow rather than something sinister beating a path through it.

If she told herself that often enough, she might even believe it.

The dark gray stone front of the house was clear enough even through a crisscrossing network of vines. Pulling all of that mess off without getting a ripping case of poison ivy or encountering angry wasps or even copperheads didn't seem likely.

Three stone chimneys jutted up from the black shingled roof, looking more or less intact. Same with several windows, including a huge picture window she'd always loved. Her clearest time-fogged memories were of watching early but glorious sunsets through that window or out on the porch with her great aunt.

She couldn't say the same for the deep porch that was supposed to run the length of the house. A massive tree had fallen through the far side, leaving the gorgeous oak door stranded about fifteen feet above the ground. What looked like a mat of five-leaved Virginia creeper rather than noxious poison ivy had grown over the collapsed part and up onto the porch swing. Thank goodness it wasn't more of the relentless kudzu.

Amy wasn't sure she wanted to know what kind of miracle kept the swing's slender chains hanging on.

If she managed to summon the courage to go into the house today, it would probably have to be through the side door to the left, protected by a miniature roof on the high side of the yard. An ominous humming and barely visible darts of movement from there looked way too much like a bee colony had moved in ahead of her for comfort.

Amy had a clouded memory of some kind of basement or cellar, and a grownups-only trapdoor, but she didn't even know where to start looking.

Speaking of roofs, the main one seemed intact as far as her inexpert eye could tell, black shingles smooth and unbroken. Almost like new. But she assumed it would need work soon after who knew how many years of neglect. Along with everything else Amy saw, and the other stuff she didn't know to look for yet.

Work a long-time apartment dweller had no idea how to even get started.

Hadn't Mr. Steffens mentioned something about a maintenance fund? Or a payout? Or at least a bank account? Amy had notes and paperwork back in the tiny car, but the idea of hiking back down there, getting bad news, and then having to slog right back up here was more than she could stand.

Tapping into her meager savings to repair a house she wasn't sure she wanted—and when she hadn't yet found a long-term rental in Chicago after the break-up—was even worse.

Amy let out an honest to goodness, grown-ass-woman scream when someone spoke from right behind her.

Chapter 2

"Sorry I'm so late getting over here to meet you."

Amy spun around, *almost* keeping her balance in the weeds that chose that moment to grasp at her ankles. The strange woman reached out to steady her. Amy could only hope the woman didn't notice when she drew back and almost fell anyway.

Being touched by strangers was hardly her favorite thing. Even if they hadn't crept up and scared her half to death.

"Late meeting me? I don't understand. Who are you?"

The woman brushed at her short shag of shiny black hair, then at her long-sleeved denim shirt. She was several inches taller than Amy, with broad shoulders and a solid, comfortable way of standing. Her face was pale and heart-shaped, and Amy had the strangest feeling she should have recognized those dark blue, almost violet eyes.

"I'm Melissa Phillips, but most folks call me Missy."

For a second Amy was certain she'd misheard, probably because the scare still had her heart thumping in her ears.

"Phillips," she said. "You don't mean the family who lives just over the mountain?"

She *didn't* say: The ones who helped keep this house and land tied up in court and drove my family nuts with a bunch of bullshit property and boundary claims all these years. Maybe put my Great Auntie Maybelle in her grave sooner than she should have been.

Apparently Amy didn't need to say it. Missy Phillips blushed pink from her throat to her hairline.

"That's some of my people, yeah. Hardly any of that bunch left now. I'm the only one that stays up here, getting the old place fixed up a little. Hope to find somewhere else before the weather turns cold."

She held out her hand, large but delicate. Amy hesitated as she always did with the uncomfortable social ritual, then managed a quick handshake. Missy's grip was firm, her palm warm and calloused.

"This might sound strange," Amy said, "but I keep thinking I should know you."

Missy nodded, then flashed a shy smile.

"We crossed paths a good bit, sure. Back when we were kids. At the park in town, up on this mountain running around. For what it's worth, I always did like Maybelle."

Long-unused memory circuits sparked and jumped back into life, and Amy couldn't hide her own smile.

"I *do* remember you. Your hair was really long back then, wasn't it? Down to…"

Missy laughed, sounding remarkably like a songbird.

"I heard a few less than friendly kids say it was down to my ass and back. I'd guess that's what you're trying to call to mind."

Now Amy covered her smile with one hand, wishing she could cover her whole face. She did remember that rather unkind phrase, and a fascinating, tiny little girl with dark blue eyes who got downright angry about it. Amy wished she didn't remember the words quite so well.

"I really hope I wasn't one of those kids," Amy said. "I wasn't, was I?"

Missy shook her head, but she looked away from Amy and up at the house.

"If you ever said it, I don't remember. My daddy wouldn't let anyone cut my hair when I was a kid. He even kept it brushed and braided for years when my mother refused but I couldn't manage it yet. That's one reason I took to hacking it off myself when I turned fifteen. Still do sometimes."

"I remember how pretty your hair was," Amy said. Heat surged up from her belly when she realized more than one way that sounded strange. "I mean, it's still pretty now. Mine gets on my last nerve sometimes and it's only halfway down my back."

Missy nodded toward Amy. "Yours is right pretty, too. Always was. Listen, I was real sorry to hear about your folks. Losing both of them at the same time like that must have been tough."

Amy blinked, surprised to feel the first real stab of grief over her parents in years. Maybe because Missy actually knew them, unlike most people Amy spent time with now. That day in her twenties when a car crash took them both honestly felt like another lifetime.

"Thank you, I appreciate that. It was a rough couple of years for sure. How are your parents?"

Missy shrugged with one shoulder, shaking her head.

"Daddy's out in Hidden Springs at the assisted living, has been for years. I was a surprise after they thought having kids was over with, so he's in his eighties. My mother is long gone."

"I'm so sorry to hear that, Missy. We're too young to be down to just one parent between us, huh?"

"Just the way it worked out," Missy said with a tight

smile. "Looks like you already have the house keys. Been inside yet?"

Amy jingled the keys in her hand for some absurd reason.

"I haven't been inside since I was eleven years old. Have you?"

Missy shrugged. "Not for a long time. I helped out Maybelle as much as I could when she was still alive. When I could slip over here without anyone else knowing."

Amy took a deep breath, concentrating on sweet honeysuckle and the rich scent of the forest nearby.

Missy seemed nice enough now, and if Amy was remembering right she'd been a real sweetheart when they were kids. But all the nonsense that kept this property from being lived in or even maintained for decades was surely dangerous ground between them. Especially when Amy was faced with having to decide what to do with it now.

"I don't think anyone's been here for a long time. I appreciate you helping my great aunt out. I really do. You're here because Mr. Steffens asked you to meet me?"

Missy took a step back, and Amy felt the air between them turn colder.

"I would have if Mr. Steffens asked. Truth is I volunteered. I wanted to help. Once I knew someone was finally going to be taking care of the place, I figured it was the least I could do."

"This is the first time any of us have had a *chance* to take care of the place," Amy snapped, and regretted it immediately. "I'm sorry. I didn't know anything about any of this until a few days ago, and I've been up since five this morning. Thank you for meeting me, Missy."

Missy tilted her head a few degrees to the side and looked into Amy's eyes for a long moment. Amy did her best to return the gaze without any kind of built up hostility from a feud she never had quite understood.

"Maybe we should just see if we can get one of the doors open." She walked past Amy and toward the house without a backward glance.

Chapter 3

By the time Amy caught up to Missy's determined, steady stride through all the vines, weeds, and clouds of tiny bugs hovering in annoying bunches, Missy stood several steps back from the side door and the small overhanging roof. The buzzing swarm of much larger insects didn't seem to bother her at all.

They bothered Amy. A lot.

"Are those honeybees?" Amy said.

Missy nodded, not turning away from the swarming yellow and black creatures.

"That's right. Seem to have a pretty good size colony going. Probably getting a good load of honey on this time of year."

Amy ducked and stepped back when three of the bees took off and flew way too close to her head. She tried to remember if she had her prescription antihistamines in her hastily packed suitcase.

"But where? Are they living inside the house?"

Missy stepped forward, not seeming to mind one bit that her own head was now inside the bee flight path.

"Looks like they found a crack in the stones here. That or some missing grout. Can't tell if they're inside or just in the wall."

Amy stood with her hands on her hips, trying not to either scream or cry. Her reaction generally wasn't EpiPen or emergency room severe, but she had no desire to test it out here in the middle of nowhere. As far as she knew or remembered, getting to the nearest hospital would easily take an hour.

"Well, I can't go in this way," she said a bit too loudly. "Even if one of this bunch of keys doesn't open any other door."

Missy turned, looking Amy in the eye. She didn't look disdainful or mean. Only curious.

"Allergic or just scared?"

"Allergic. So, yes, that means I do my best to avoid getting stung." Amy held out the bundle of keys. "The front porch is probably out until I can find someone who knows how to repair it. Do you have any idea what all these other keys are even *for*?"

Missy took the keys, still holding Amy's gaze. Once again embarrassed at how sharp her voice sounded, Amy turned away, staring out toward the kudzu ruin of the barn and her invisible rental car lost in a sea of shifting green.

Being tired and unprepared—and blindsided by family history that had mainly taken place without her—didn't give her an excuse for being rude to the one person who might be willing to help her. Or at least to try.

She turned back at a shake of the keys. Missy jerked her chin around toward the back of the house.

"Should be able to get in through the root cellar if you're up for that. I don't know if the old trapdoor up into the house is clear or not. Last few times I visited with Maybelle, she had me fetch things out of the cellar for her and bring them around by the outside. She had the trapdoor blocked."

"Blocked? How? Did she say why? She loved that thing when I was last here."

Missy took a slow, deep breath, rolling her lips in between her teeth, then over to the side. Amy couldn't help noticing how full and nicely shaped they were.

"I don't want to stir up any more bad feelings between us," Missy said. "Not when I already did that without meaning to."

Amy glanced at the bees, then took a step closer. She was gratified when Missy closed the distance by walking away from the swarm.

"It's okay, Missy. I'm not in any state to be around people, really. I should pack it in for the night and try again tomorrow. I know Great Auntie Maybelle had trouble toward the end. I was too young to understand much. I guess you were, too."

"Maybe. I know I got my bottom smacked for sneaking over here those last few times. I guess I felt bad about all the… Never mind that. What Maybelle told me was something tried to get up through the floor, so she wanted it blocked. Or she might have said something tried to get *out* through the floor, can't remember for sure. Anyway, she had someone haul one of those huge wardrobes over top of the trapdoor."

At the thought of her sweet Great Auntie Maybelle—always so ready with a broad smile and a big hug and a kiss—being frightened and paranoid and so alone, Amy had officially had enough for the day.

"Okay. I understand. I'm glad you where there when… when she needed someone." Amy refused to dwell on why her own family hadn't been there. "I am going to call it a night. Maybe we can try the whole thing again in the morning. Around ten?"

Missy nodded and dropped the keys into Amy's hand.

"You staying with family in town?"

Amy let out a harsh bark of a laugh.

"You see any of them up here helping me with all this? I have a room at the new hotel."

"There's the one thing we have in common, I guess. Won't catch me around my people much either. Not if I can help it. Get some rest."

Chapter 4

THE NEXT MORNING turned out much cooler, with heavy gray clouds covering what little sky Amy could see from her great aunt's house. *Her* house, at least for now. Maybe if she focused on that little bit, she'd eventually get used to the whole thing.

Worried about the rain leaving the overgrown driveway too muddy for her little car to navigate, she didn't drive nearly as far up the road before she parked. But far enough along the tunnel of huge oaks, poplars, and maples so no one would see a strange car and get curious.

A bunch of strangers wandering around and asking questions was the last thing Amy felt up to dealing with. She'd been craving a break from crowds of strangers every time she walked down the street for a long time now, even if she missed other kinds of company more than she wanted to admit.

The walk up felt as different as the weather. Today she smelled trees and soil and every green thing, stirred up somehow, waiting on the storms to get there. Even the massive kudzu leaves covering the remains of the barn just past her car seemed turned up and eager.

Almost all the buzzing insects had fallen silent along with the squirrels. Only the distant crows fussing and squabbling broke the rustle of leaves in the constant wind, driving cool damp air in a rush across the land.

A few uninterrupted hours of sleep—aided by earplugs and melatonin—left Amy with enough presence of mind to buy a pair of bright yellow umbrellas on the way through town. She'd even managed to stock up on water and a good bunch of chips, soda, and hard candy.

She didn't expect Missy or herself to do the serious work ahead to get the old Johnstone home place into livable or even visitable condition. But the least Amy could do after being so snappish and weird the day before was make an effort to be hospitable.

Even though she did her best to keep an ear out for Missy, Amy still jumped when she spoke.

"Don't know how much time we'll be able to get in before that storm breaks."

This time Missy stood at the corner of the house past the side door, hand on her hips, staring up at the lowering clouds. She wore her same blue jeans and denim shirt outfit, and her thick black hair gleamed in the low light.

"I don't know how much the two of us can do besides get one of the doors open," Amy said. "How do you *do* that? Show up without making a sound, I mean?"

Missy snorted. "I never was good at walking around without making a bunch of noise. Not compared to some of my people. Must be noisy wherever you live now."

Amy nodded, forcing herself not to talk about the uncomfortable silence of her anonymous short-term-stay apartment, the sensible option while she looked for a new place of her own. The depressing lack of people who weren't strangers in her daily life.

Generally, the lack of what she used to think of as the annoying background hum of co-workers, going about their workdays and getting on her last fragile nerve. That clatter and clutter and chatter that she missed terribly now that she'd been "promoted" to a remote job and worked full-time from home.

Specifically, the lack of people named Cindy who'd shared Amy's bed in their cozy apartment what seemed like a hundred years ago now.

In her heart, it felt like five minutes ago half the time, to be painfully honest.

"The city can get noisy, sure," she said. "But you're not nearly as loud as you think. Figure anything out about that trapdoor?"

Missy jerked her chin toward the back of the house, then turned and started walking.

"I reckon the best thing is if one of us can get in through these windows back here. That way if the trapdoor *is* blocked, we can get it cleared out. I know people who will come out here and collect your bee colony and get it relocated. For free, even, since they keep the queen and all."

"Good. If you could please get me their number I'll call them. I won't be able to sell this place or move in or anything else with a giant hive of bees built into the wall."

The gray stone around the back side of the house wasn't interrupted by nearly so many windows, and somehow none of them were broken. The view of the tree-covered hillside close by wasn't nearly as enticing as the valley and higher mountains out front. The steps and break in the wall of the cellar waited several paces farther along.

Missy glanced back at Amy. "I'll tell them about the bees.

They can be funny about strangers, like a lot of people back in here can."

"I'm not exactly a stranger," Amy said without thinking. "I was born just down the road."

Missy stopped in front of two windows that Amy thought opened into the kitchen. She didn't move from her hands-on-hips stance or look at Amy when she spoke.

"I know you were born here. But anyone younger than what, thirty? They never would have met you. That makes you a stranger to them."

She stepped forward and tried to rattle the waist-high window in its frame. White paint peeled off the wooden frame and trim pieces, but the panes were sturdy.

Amy decided not to respond to that last bit about being a stranger. The truth was she would probably sell this place as soon as she could get it cleaned up, and then she'd *be* a stranger. She hadn't exaggerated about not being in touch with her local family.

She hadn't tried to keep up with them any more than they'd kept up with her.

And once this was all finished and behind her, she doubted she'd be making any more effort to keep in touch with Missy.

So what they thought of each other besides foggy childhood memories was irrelevant.

Right?

"I guess I ought to ask since you're the owner now," Missy said, stepping over to check the next window. "These are solid and locked. How do you feel about breaking one of them?"

"Not great. But we need to get inside somehow. How do you feel about trying to climb up on what's left of the porch?"

Missy let out that sweet songbird laughter again.

"I don't feel too great about that, either. Not until I can get back over here with better tools. Want to do the honors?"

It took Amy a few seconds to realize Missy was asking her if she wanted to break the window. To break the window in her own house, actually. On purpose.

She couldn't stop herself from grinning.

"I've never done anything like breaking a window on purpose in my life. Never broke one accidentally, either. Should I just throw a rock?"

Missy laughed under her breath, shaking her head.

"Why sure, if you want to. Might be a lot less glass to clean up if you tap the window instead, but you're the boss. I can get it fixed right up for you either way."

"You can fix it? Old window glass like this?"

Missy nodded, smiling.

"Sure can, and your porch. Just about anything else, too. I work carpentry and construction. I see a lot of old houses like this all over Boun County. Been making sure the roof is sound over here for years now, keeping an eye on the windows and such."

"You've been repairing the roof?" Amy said. "Mr. Steffens didn't mention anything about that. This will probably make me sound dumber than I feel, but aren't roofs expensive?"

"The supplies came out of the maintenance account set up in Maybelle's will. I wanted to do it, or I wouldn't have bothered."

Amy forced herself not to argue or try to make Missy take more money for her work. Her pride that felt stung at the idea of being a stranger knew Missy's pride wouldn't take well to an offer of payment.

"Well, I'm glad to know there's some kind of money to get this place fixed up," Amy said. "Thank you for keeping the roof in good shape, Missy."

Missy nodded once with a quick smile.

She turned in a circle looking for a rock, then handed Amy a chunk of limestone that fit perfectly in her palm.

"Probably should have safety glasses or something," Missy said, stepping back. "But we'll make do. Just turn your head to the side and have at it."

Amy hefted the rock, jagged and cool and heavier than it looked. The insanity of the past few days, much less the last several months, had her tempted to throw it as hard as she could and damn the consequences.

But a vivid image of the rock bouncing off the stone wall instead, maybe hard enough to fly back and hit her in her own damn fool forehead, made her walk up to the window.

A few taps on individual panes had the house accessible with much less drama, though it was definitely less satisfying.

A musty smell wafted out into the cooling, humid air, but not nearly as strong and thick as Amy expected.

She remembered Missy saying her Auntie might have been trying to keep something from getting into the house through the cellar. Or *out* through the cellar.

She shivered, not sure which would be worse.

"Think I can get inside if you give me a boost," Missy said. "You can go first if you want. Is the electricity on?"

"I couldn't get it turned back on yet. It's been off long enough that they want to inspect it first, make sure everything is up to code. You know more about that since you work construction. No one can make it out here to do that until day after tomorrow. Can you see what's under the window? I'd hate for either one of us to land on a china cabinet or in a sink."

She pulled out her phone and thumbed on the flashlight, surprised for some reason to see Missy doing the same thing. They stood nearly shoulder to shoulder and peered inside.

"Looks like a table," Missy said. "Should be sturdy enough."

The lights cut through floating dust to hit a dark, reddish wooden table that Amy remembered well. Neither beam reached much beyond the surface. Only enough to see three matching curved-back chairs tucked in close, and thick shadows.

"That's her breakfast table, the one my Great Uncle Harmon made for her. Or it was. I guess it's mine now. It's plenty sturdy if I'm remembering right. He made it out of cherry wood for their anniversary a few years before he died, and Great Auntie Maybelle kept it polished like a mirror. I barely remember him at all. I wish we had brighter lights than this. I didn't plan ahead all that well."

Missy stepped back, turning her phone off and slipping it into her pants pocket. Thunder rumbled toward the front of the house.

"I didn't plan so good either, and I more or less knew what we were getting into. I can bring something stronger tomorrow or later today. Maybe once this storm passes over. Maybelle used to have oil lamps stored back everywhere. Might find a couple of those once we get inside."

"I remember those," Amy said, smiling. "Seemed like the power was off all the time up here. I loved it when Great Auntie Maybelle lit up all those lamps." She made a quick decision, not quite ready to face her memories or her ghosts alone. "You can go in first if you don't mind."

Instead of questioning, Missy stepped forward and settled her hands on the opening in the stones, carefully avoiding the glass. Amy bent over, lacing her fingers together to make a step. With less effort than she expected, Missy was over the edge and inside.

Amy saw her crouch on the table for a second, then the phone light flipped on again.

"I'll see if I can get to the trapdoor. One of your keys should open the lock on the cellar door."

She scooted forward and disappeared into the darkness.

Chapter 5

AMY HESITATED FOR A SECOND, trying to recall the last time she'd been inside the house. So many visits over so many years blended together in her mind. She wasn't sure what day it was, what they'd talked about. Even what season it had been. Whatever happened, she'd had no idea how much time would pass between visits. Or that she'd never see her beloved great aunt again.

And her eleven-year-old self had no way to imagine how many secrets and surprises her forty-one-year-old mind and heart would hold.

Several layers of leaves and grass and even moss were built up on the cellar steps, so much so that weeds had taken root. A rumble of thunder loud enough to rattle those solid windows passed overhead while Amy fumbled for the key.

She couldn't remember ever seeing a lock on the cellar door, but the rusted chunk of what felt like solid steel had to be decades old. Ancient enough that she was halfway convinced the conventional keys she had wouldn't do the job at all.

Surely it would take some kind of elaborate skeleton key,

one longer than her whole hand, to fit into the bottom of the massive lock and coax it open. But only if she whispered the proper magic spell at the same time under the light of the full moon.

The fourth key, a simple silvery one that didn't look quite as aged as the others, did the trick just as she heard Missy's voice through the door.

"Making any progress out there? I'm about ready to get out of this cellar now."

Amy yanked the lock away from the equally reluctant loop of metal, creating a disturbingly lifelike shriek. The reluctant shift of wood that hadn't moved for most of her lifetime was almost as noisy.

Missy blinked up at her, wearing several smudges of dirt and what looked like soot on her face and hands.

Amy took the last few steps down into the cellar. She got a bit wobbly on a loose stone and grabbed Missy's outstretched hand without thinking. Her normal dislike of touching strangers got swept away in a flush of heat.

"Did you have to move the wardrobe?" Amy said.

"It was already shoved back." Missy opened her mouth, then closed it hard enough to click her teeth together. "You'll see when you get up there."

Amy stopped herself from asking a bunch more questions, nothing more than an attempt to stall her walk through the house.

This cellar barely registered on her nostalgia meter. It was all concrete and cinderblocks, sharp angles and the same scary oil furnace she never did like as a kid.

Upstairs the real sorrow and guilt would likely surge up and try to drown her if she gave it the chance.

"Might want to pull the door to," Missy said, stepping toward it. "If that storm dumps a whole lot of rain, leaving it open might make a mess of this cellar."

"I remember that part." Amy joined Missy, then kicked away the leaves and especially thick coat of green moss at the sides of the bottom step. A dark circle in each corner led down and out of sight. "Special drains to keep the water from building up. I never liked this cellar, but those drains fascinated me. And unless someone moved it…"

Amy leaned to her right and reached into a ridge in the rocks along the edge of the door. Partly natural from the way the squared-off stones had been laid out, partly hollowed out by her father and who knew who all else.

Her bee-spooked mind conjured visions of hornets and wasps and spiders and everything else that could possibly sting crouching just out of sight, stingers poised and ready.

Instead she pulled out a black metal pipe as long as her arm with three smaller pipes at a ninety degree angle at the end.

"What on earth *is* that thing?" Missy said, crossing her arms.

"I don't know what it was supposed to be. Maybe something for a fireplace or a wood stove. We always used it to dig down and clear these drains if they got clogged. Maybe once in a while to chase each other around with." Amy tucked the drain cleaner back into its spot.

"Glad no one ever got it out when I was over here."

They pulled the door closed and each grabbed for their phones again. Even with the power out and the last oil probably drained before she was in high school, Amy had no desire to get close to the hulking black furnace. She walked behind Missy so she could avoid it without being observed.

The concrete continued into a flight of wide stairs against one wall, the edges as sharp as when they were poured. Only a thick coat of dust and ropes of cobwebs in the corners marked the time passing.

"It's all in pretty good shape down here," Amy said. "Maybe that luck will hold with the rest of the house."

Missy glanced back over her shoulder, eyes narrowed a bit but not giving a thing away. She led the way up the stairs and through the open trapdoor and into the darkness above.

When Amy stepped up onto the lovely old hardwood floor, she scowled at a curving set of deep gouges in the wide boards. She started to stay something to Missy, but stopped cold at the look on her face.

Missy's full lips were compressed, and her eyebrows drawn down toward her dark blue eyes. She didn't look angry, though, like Amy had just been.

Missy looked afraid.

"What did–" Amy started, then her gaze followed Missy's.

She breathed in a sharp gasp of the thick, musty air.

Gouges weren't the only thing marking the floor.

Chapter 6

THE HALLWAY here at the end of the house was several paces wide, with doors on both sides leading to small bedrooms with open doors. A bathroom door stood open at the very end. All the heavy curtains were drawn tight, without even a tiny sliver of light getting through.

One of her Great Auntie Maybelle's huge oak wardrobes was shoved back against the wall beside one of the bedrooms. The legs matched the gouges on the floor perfectly.

And all over the floor, cutting through the heavy layer of dust, footprints stood out.

Countless footprints.

Amy saw Missy's work boot prints over top of the others, clearly the most recent. Coming from the kitchen, turning in a circle, then disappearing down into the cellar.

But more shapes and sizes of footprints than Amy could fit into her reeling mind spread out from there. The undeniable marks of the heels and toes of bare feet, in every size from what looked like a tiny baby all the way up to prints so large they looked unreal.

Some so flat the whole foot showed. Others with an arch

as high as Amy's, with only the barest outline of flesh between toes and heel.

Footprints from each of the bedrooms, into and out of the bathroom. Footprints going to and from the kitchen and the living room beyond. So many going right up to the trapdoor to the cellar that the wood was almost rubbed clean of dust.

Amy's heart thudded in her chest as she slowly looked back up. Missy's mouth and eyes turned down now, like she was was fighting back tears. Or a scream.

"What is all this?" Amy said, her voice wavering in time with her heart.

Missy shook her head. "I never saw the like. Goes all through the house as far as I could see."

Amy stared toward the kitchen again, more aware of the darkness as a nearly physical thing than she ever had been in her life. If their phones lost power, she truly wouldn't be able to see an inch in front of her face.

"You said the doors were locked up tight," Amy said. "The windows, too."

Missy nodded.

"Then who did this? When?"

"If I had any idea I'd sure tell you, Amy. You saw the windows and doors same as I did. All I can tell you is no one's been inside that I know of. But this place sure is in better shape than it has any right to be after all this time."

Shivers vibrated through Amy's whole body, not much different than during a bone-chilling cold snap in Chicago.

How much did she actually know about Missy? They'd gotten along all those years ago, been pretty close the more Amy thought about it. But she hadn't seen or heard anything about Missy since then.

She'd heard plenty about Missy's family, though. None of

it good, and almost all of it having to do with the house they stood in.

The house full of footprints that didn't make any damn sense.

Hell, Amy hadn't even bothered to contact Art Steffens last night or this morning, to at least make sure Missy really had let him know she'd volunteered to come up here to help. Not that anyone's phone got even a ghost of a signal up here.

And right now, all Missy had to do was kick the trapdoor closed, knock the phone out of her hand, and Amy would *be* well and truly trapped. Missy looked plenty strong enough to do that and not even break a sweat.

Assuming they weren't *both* trapped with at least one of the people who'd made those damn footprints.

"Okay then," Amy said, waving a shaking hand toward the floor. "Who do you think did this? And what we should do about it?"

Missy shook her head, turning to shine her phone's light into one of the bedrooms. Both of them jumped when the beam reflected off a mirror.

"I'm not about to guess on who or *what* made these tracks. As far as what we should do, get the hell out and come back with the police? Or a preacher? Or better yet both, but not until the electric's back on?"

A high-pitched, potentially manic giggle escaped Amy. The terrifying sound of it echoing through the empty house stopped every trace of humor cold.

What if she kept laughing like that and some unseen creature laughed back?

"Should we... Maybe we should open the curtains at least? Try to get some daylight in here?"

A sharp, gigantic clap of thunder overhead forced grunts out of both of them. Her earlier doubts shoved aside, Amy now figured Missy was too scared to scream. Just like she was herself.

"I think we just ran out of daylight," Missy said. A thick rumble of rain on the roof backed her up. "Might not be so easy to get out of here for a while, either."

"How did you get over here?" Amy hoped the answer would be something sensible like a four-wheeler.

"I walked over on the old trail across the mountain. A lot shorter than the road." They both jumped again at another huge burst of thunder, and Missy glanced up at the ceiling. "I wouldn't want to walk out under a bunch of trees with this kind of storm going."

Realizing all at once that the noisy rain kept them from hearing anyone or anything that might be moving around inside the house, Amy rubbed her own arms.

"I don't think I want to stay inside here, either," she said. "How do you feel about the cellar instead?"

"Not my favorite idea, to tell you the truth. But not quite as bad as I feel about standing around up here without more light than this. Maybelle used to keep a couple of those lanterns in her bedroom. Want to wait here while I get one?"

Amy again fought back manic laughter.

"You think I'm going to spend one second in this house alone? I don't know how the hell you made it from the kitchen back here."

Missy flashed a quick grin.

"Honestly? I didn't notice the floor until I went to open the trapdoor. By then I was too damn scared to turn around. Just about broke my neck running down the stairs. If you hadn't got the cellar door open when you did I was gonna hunt for an axe or something like it to start breaking my way out."

"Okay then," Amy said, trying to make her voice sound

more confident than she felt. "We'll get a couple of lanterns and go back downstairs."

She forced herself not to look around one more time, not to keep glancing back over her shoulder. If she started that, she'd still be standing here scared to death when the sun came up in the morning.

The inside of her Great Auntie Maybelle's bedroom was eerily unchanged under the dust and more cobwebs. Same queen-sized bed set under the window. Same beautiful crazy quilt made up of dozens of fabric scraps, none bigger than a few inches across. Same blue paisley pattern curtain hanging across the closet built against the wall to the right, an odd little room-within-a-room that didn't quite reach to the ceiling.

The glaring change was all the footprints going from the closet to the bed and out the door.

Amy gasped when Missy touched her shoulder.

"Sorry about that," Missy said. "The lanterns are still there."

Missy's phone light pointed to the top of the afterthought closet and sparkled off two old-fashioned curvy oil lamps. The bases were made of ornate blue glass that narrowed down to the metal piece that held the white fabric wick, then the clear glass chimney flared back out in the middle. Amy thought it was just as well that the matching blue globes sat off to the side. Those things were far too easy to break.

"The matches were in her dresser drawer, right?" Amy said, walking to the Art Deco style dresser. She carefully avoided looking into the huge oval mirror, too terrified of seeing someone besides herself and Missy looking back at her. "Yep, got 'em."

She slipped a small rectangular match box into her pocket, hoping it hadn't been in the drawer so long that they wouldn't strike any more. She also hoped Missy would volunteer to retrieve the oil lamps.

The thought of standing in front of that closet curtain, stretching up and having to lean close to a space she couldn't see, chilled Amy to the bone.

"I'll step up in the dresser chair," Missy said, "if you don't mind. Since you own the place."

"Since all I want to do is get out of this house as fast as I possibly can, I don't mind one bit. I'll even hold the chair for you."

Amy did her best to keep her eyes away from the curtain, with the added challenge of trying not to stare at Missy's rather distracting backside. Missy had set her phone down on the bed with the light tilted toward the closet.

Inadvertently putting her own anatomy in the spotlight.

Even through Missy's blue jeans and the prickly tension in the room, Amy's favorite combination of strong and shapely was unmistakable.

So was a breeze (or something) pushing the paisley curtains forward.

Missy handed one of the oil lamps to Amy, waiting until Amy had a good grasp on the heavy glass base.

"Is there a window or something inside this closet?" Missy said.

Amy shook her head before she remembered Missy couldn't see her.

"No. Not unless it got added later on for some crazy reason. It's just the back wall. Do…do you feel that breeze, too?"

"I feel the curtain moving," Missy said. "Don't much like it."

As she handed the second oil lamp down, the curtain shifted back again, then blew straight out hard enough to wrap itself around Missy's legs.

Chapter 7

Amy shrieked and dropped the second lamp, jumping back from the glass and oil explosion. Before she could get herself more than a couple of steps toward the door, Missy pushed close and yelled from behind her.

"Go go go!"

Amy ran out and down the cellar stairs, clutching the remaining oil lamp to her chest with both arms. Thankfully Missy had managed to grab her phone on the way out, lighting the path ahead.

The crashing slam of the trapdoor was only a little bit louder than the thunder.

Missy stood at the foot of the concrete stairs, panting, hands on her knees, eyes locked on the path they'd just taken.

"What the *hell* was that?" Amy shouted. She backed up against the cellar door to the outside, somehow still holding on to the lamp.

"Damned if I know. Swear those curtains tried to grab me."

"Can you lock the trapdoor? Keep whatever it is from getting down here?"

Missy straightened up, still staring up at the ceiling.

"With what? I doubt there's a lock on it, or any kind of loops I could jam something through. I was moving too fast to do a careful inspection. Let's see if we can get that lamp lit. At least save our phone's batteries."

Amy carefully set the lamp down on the concrete floor and squatted beside it.

"Save them for what?" she said. "There's not a scrap of signal anywhere out here, certainly not down in this basement."

She lifted the chimney off the lamp, not liking how badly her hand shook. Getting a match struck was going to be a trick, much less lighting a wick that had to be decades old. Thankfully a couple of inches of oil stood in the bottom.

Missy shrugged and took a couple of steps toward Amy. Amy was amazed to still hear thunder down in the cellar.

"I don't know, just in case this storm doesn't let up and we have to stay down here for a while. Tell me the truth, Amy. Did you ever hear anyone in your family talk about this place being haunted?"

"Haunted?" Amy paused with one of the precious matches in her fingertips, staring at Missy. "I never heard anything like that. I haven't exactly been in close touch with most of my family for a long time, remember? They could have had some ghost hunter show out here three times a year for the last ten and I never would have known. Have *you* heard anything like that?"

Missy stepped closer again, still watching the stairs.

"I never did hear haunted, no," Missy said. "Nothing like that. Pretty much everyone down in Bountyfield seems to have forgotten this place ever existed, and I make sure to never remind them. That's probably why no one comes up here to make a mess. As far as my family, more like a bunch of ancestral land nonsense that I never paid much attention to."

"None of this answers where all those footprints came from. Or what made those curtains blow out like that."

Amy was amazed that the first match actually flared and lit, and even more so when the lamp's wick caught. She adjusted the flat white fabric rope nearly level with the metal dispenser, then settled the chimney into place. A warm, cheery glow entirely at odds with how she was feeling filled part of the cellar.

"I wish I had answers for you, Amy, I truly do. This is the first time I've set foot inside this house for almost thirty years myself. All I ever did was scramble around on the roof. Pretty sure I'd remember mysterious footprints all over the place if I'd seen them when Maybelle was still alive."

A muted thud sounded over their heads, far too small and quiet to be thunder. Chills raced across Amy's skin.

"Did you…" she whispered.

Missy nodded.

Another thud.

And the much softer thump-squeak, thump-squeak of someone walking barefoot on a hardwood floor.

Someone making no effort whatsoever to be quiet or sneaky about it.

"What the *hell*?" Amy said. "Are you sure there's no way to lock that trapdoor?"

Missy's eyes were wide, her mouth drawn back in horror.

"I said I didn't think there was a lock. Didn't see one. Maybe we should just take our chances with the storm."

"Yeah, I'm good with that, Missy. But if we can lock it, we probably should. I don't want whatever that is getting out of the house, do you?"

Missy took a deep breath, clenching her fists.

"Not when it's just over the mountain from where I've

been staying. Come on, bring your phone. And your keys. We can both make sure there's not a lock or some way to jam it shut."

The sounds of slow pacing continued above their heads, but Amy managed to get unsteadily to her feet. Every nerve and muscle in her body demanded she get out and leave the house to its own devices.

But she also felt an odd and unwelcome sense of responsibility for whatever was happening.

And the bone-deep certainty that leaving the trapdoor unlocked would be a very bad thing.

Both lights jittered as they walked closer, and Amy was unhappy to have to walk up a few steps before the beams reached the trapdoor.

"There!" Missy pointed. "There *is* a lock, hanging on the right."

Amy's light picked out a shape dark and rusty enough to nearly blend into the floor beams. Smaller and flatter than the huge one on the outside of the cellar, but clearly a padlock. She couldn't think of a sensible reason for the trapdoor to be locked from this side, but someone else clearly had.

At least two sets of feet walked overhead now, the second with a much faster, lighter pace than the first.

"We should hurry if…if we're gonna do this," Amy said. "My heart's about to pound out of my chest."

"Sounds like they're walking in circles. Maybe they don't know we're down here. Get ready to hand me those keys in case it's closed for some dumb reason."

The two of them walked slowly up the stairs. Amy felt disconnected from her own body, hard trembling working to cut off her arms and legs from her brain. She held the keys gripped tight in one hand to stop them from jingling, her phone's light pointed at the lock in the other.

The few seconds of their climb added another pattern upstairs; a heavier step with what sounded like a drag in the middle.

As Missy reached for the padlock, Amy wanted to cry out in relief. The lock's body hung over to the side, with the curved arm open and through a thick metal ring set into a wooden beam at least eight inches thick.

The pacing stopped the second Missy touched the lock.

Missy shook her head and started to back down.

"No, we're right here," Amy whispered. "Just push it closed."

She slipped the keys into her pocked and touched Missy's back. Her muscles felt like a human-sized tuning fork, struck hard and vibrating fast.

Missy reached up with both hands and lifted the curved shackle enough to push it through the matching metal ring on the bottom of the trapdoor.

When she turned the body of the lock, trying to line it up so she could push it closed, it broke loose with a harsh, metallic squeak.

Footsteps thundered over their heads.

"It's jammed!" Missy shouted. "It won't close!"

"Give it a good shove. Even if it won't lock, at least it's through those rings."

The pounding seemed to come from all over the house, but Amy was certain it was circling closer to the trapdoor.

Chapter 8

Missy turned the lock back and forth, lined it up again, and set the heel of her hand against the rusty bottom. When she pushed again with both hands, putting her whole body behind the effort, it finally snapped closed.

Now dust and grit filtered down from the trapdoor inches over their heads.

Amy grabbed Missy's hand and they dashed back down to the cellar floor.

When they got to the door, Amy turned back.

"The lamp. I should—

"You should *leave* it. Might be best for everyone if this damn place burns down!"

Missy yanked the cellar door open, letting in a gush of leaf and dirt filled water. The drains at the bottom of the steps had clogged after all.

They only hesitated long enough to pull the door around and jam the padlock closed before they ran out into the pouring rain and toward the driveway.

Both skidded to a muddy stop at the sight of Amy's little rental car, dwarfed by the massive crown of an oak tree right behind it. Small branches and vines trailed across the driveway where the damaging wind had torn through.

No trace of burning wood smell from a lighting strike. Only the fresh ozone scent of the rain and the storm.

Whatever remained of the old kudzu-covered barn had been demolished when the giant fell.

"This just keeps getting better and better," Amy said, glancing back over her shoulder even though the house was hidden from view. "I'm starting to think the house or whatever's inside it doesn't want us to leave. Don't suppose you have a chainsaw with you or anything like that."

Missy shook her head as she ran one hand through her close-cropped black hair. Both women were soaked through and the rain showed no signs of letting up. At least the thunder and lightning had moved on over the ridgeline.

"Nothing with me," Missy said. "At the house, sure. Quite a slog to get over there in all this mess."

"Doesn't look like we're going anywhere else. Not unless you want to make yourself at home in that rental car. I can grab us a couple of umbrellas, though. Food too. Well, junk food. I totally forgot about that."

Amy got the door open and rummaged through the car, extremely aware of her own backside right in Missy's view. Sitting when she was dripping wet didn't seem like the best idea, though it was surely better than hiking across the mountain with the way this day was going.

She wasn't sure whether she hoped Missy was paying attention or that she wasn't.

They paused long enough for Amy to nearly inhale a small bag of salt and vinegar chips, wondering if anything on the whole planet ever tasted so good. Especially chased with a lukewarm Coke. Missy seemed every bit as satisfied with barbeque and Dr. Pepper.

Loaded up with the rest of the snacks Amy brought from

town and the painfully bright yellow umbrellas, she and Missy started back up the same driveway they'd just sprinted down.

"We don't have to get too close to the house, do we?" Amy said. She was too spooked to care how shaky her voice sounded. Not with what the two of them had experienced.

"Closer than I'd like after all that nonsense. But not right up in the yard. The trail goes off through the woods beside the house. We could walk along the road, but it adds a couple of miles and dealing with idiot drivers on wet pavement to boot. Not that many have reason to drive along that old road these days. Besides you and me, I guess. We could wait all day long out there and never see another living soul."

Amy tried her best to ignore the squishing inside her shoes, along with the way her hair, skin, and clothes were turning cold and clammy in the much cooler breeze.

She tried even harder to avoid looking at the house as they turned the corner that brought the stone wall and collapsed front porch into view. Way too much of a chance of something looking back at her.

"You said something about ancestral land earlier," she said. "What did your family say about that?"

Missy glanced at Amy, seeming more annoyed than secretive. Amy was surprised to hope Missy wasn't annoyed with *her*.

"To tell you the truth, I think one of my no-good aunts or uncles dreamed up all that ancestral land crap just to stir up more trouble. Said they'd found an old deed that proved the whole mountain was part of the original Phillips land grant, whatever that was supposed to be. Got stolen or lost again right after, of course. Not a one of the rest of us ever heard of such a thing, not before or since."

"That's what started all the legal trouble and court fights?"

Missy took a deep, slow breath.

"You really don't know much about what happened here after you left, do you?"

Amy bit back her too sharp and loud response and turned her head to the side instead. Just in time to see the wispy curtains floating outside the kitchen window

Except that window had no curtains.

And they had *broken* a window.

Chapter 9

AMY STOPPED WALKING, stopped breathing, and hoped her heart hadn't actually stopped beating.

"Missy, please look back at the house. Do you see anything strange?"

Missy stared straight ahead for several seconds, then slowly turned. Her blue eyes were again wide and frightened.

"What am I looking… Amy, the window. It's wide open."

"I would swear I just saw something moving outside of it. How far do we have to go to get cellular signal to call your police or preacher?"

"Most of the way back into town. That or a few miles up this road to the top of the ridge. We *can't* leave that window open. Not if whatever lives in that house is already trying to get out."

Shudders started up in Amy's belly again, working their way up through her arms and legs.

"No. But I don't know what we're supposed to do about it. Someone else might know what to do about…whatever this is."

Missy sat her armful of soda and snacks in a neat pile,

then arranged her open umbrella over top of it all. She didn't seem to notice the steady rain still falling, soaking through her black hair, dripping across her skin. Amy's auburn hair sat heavy, damp, and cold against her neck.

"Okay, listen," Missy said. "There was a fight over the land and the borders up here, and my idiot relatives tried their best to make it worse. But that's not what got all of this bad blood going between us. Do you remember a woman named Julie? Shorter than me, hair the same black but mostly gone to gray?"

Amy distantly realized she was backing up, getting away from the house and closer to Missy.

"Kind of. She stayed with my Great Auntie Maybelle sometimes, right?"

"That's the one. Someone in your family hired her, but not your parents. Someone their same age, probably."

Missy stopped and took a deep breath. Amy dragged her gaze away from the now-unmoving kitchen window and was startled at how pale Missy was.

"What about Julie? Who was she?"

"Whoever hired her, it was to watch over Maybelle. To help her out, drive her into town if she needed it. Well, Julie and the no-account asshole she was running around with did more than that. On one of those trips into town, they got Maybelle to change her will."

Amy couldn't possibly imagine a worse time to talk about any of this than during a rainstorm and trying to watch some unknown things that wanted to sneak out of the house.

And she couldn't imagine not knowing the whole story if she was going to have to *deal* with the house and whatever was inside.

"What? What did they do?"

"That will, it wrote your whole family out. Tried to give the land and the house and everything to Julie. That's when all the legal bullshit started and everything went to hell between our families. That's why I kept the roof up all these years. And why I jumped at the chance to help when I heard all the assholes died off and you finally ended up with the whole thing, like Maybelle wanted in the first damn place."

Amy shook her head, struggling to make sense out of a single thing about the last two days of her life.

"I still don't understand what this could have to do with whatever's going on inside that house. Or why you even *care*, Missy."

Missy closed her eyes, then let her head drop toward the muddy ground, hands on her hips. She looked up and leaned her head to the side.

"Because I don't know what most people believe about a bad place or a haunted house. But I was always told—hell, I was taught—that it was usually a great wrong done by a person that made a place bad. You know the house wasn't always like this, not when Maybelle was alive. Something *happened* here, Amy. Maybe something that can be made right."

She took a deep breath, glanced at the house, and looked back at Amy.

"And I care because Julie was my mother."

Amy's jaw dropped, and another room in her closed off chambers of memories opened wide. Missy with her beautiful down-to-her-ass-and-back hair, out in town, following along behind a woman who looked a whole lot like her.

A woman who smiled constantly at Amy's parents and at her Great Auntie Maybelle. But glared and glowered at Amy and all the rest of the cousins and other kids.

And the much younger version of Missy never did talk much or even smile at Amy when she was with that woman. Like her whole world had turned dark and lonely.

"Why didn't anyone in my family tell me about any of

this?" Amy said. She wasn't sure if the tears she was fighting back came from her fear and confusion, her sadness at what Missy had gone through, or her own family keeping her so terribly in the dark. "My parents never breathed a word of it."

"What did they tell you when you all moved?"

Amy shrugged. "That it was for work. I think I was too young and too scared and too excited to care much either way."

"We were both young, and it may have been for work. They sure wouldn't be the first to move off far away from here looking for better jobs. All I know is your folks moved you away not long after my mother pulled her nasty little stunt. If you could ask them, I bet they'd tell you that all went together."

Amy turned, staring at the house at the center of all that heartache and anger. She dropped all her snacks and the umbrella in a much less neat or organized pile than Missy had. Amy didn't see the wispy curtain thing any more, but she wasn't in a huge hurry to get back inside. Not today, and maybe not ever.

"And I never came back until yesterday," she said. "Not even one time. My Great Auntie died thinking I didn't care about her. That I didn't love her anymore."

Missy closed the distance between them and grabbed Amy's hand, her face only inches away.

"Don't you *believe* that, Amy! Not for one second. That's exactly what Julie wanted, and even years in her grave I won't let her have it! It wasn't just this land or the house. She wanted you and your parents to go away. Causing all the trouble with the law and keeping the rest of your family too upset and disgusted to interfere was a sick kind of reward for her."

Amy tried to pull her hand away but Missy wouldn't let go.

"What did she have against us? Against me? I hardly remember talking to her."

Missy reached out for Amy's other hand. After a second, Amy let her take it. Missy's hands were warm, even in the chilly rain.

And the same thrill at Missy's touch shot through Amy.

"She didn't like you," Missy said, "because of how much *I* liked you. More than I was supposed to like anyone besides her. I never did ask if she would have been as mad if it had been a boy. But looking back I don't think she would have."

"You mean you…*liked* me, liked me? Not like as a friend?"

Amy wanted to cringe at the words, but she couldn't dredge anything more sensible out of her jumbled and frightened mind.

Missy snorted out a laugh and shook her head.

"Yeah, if that's your big city way of putting it. I *liked* you, liked you. Maybe still do."

Amy opened her mouth to say she might be getting to *like* Missy too, or something equally clever and probably unbelievable.

But before she could, both she and Missy looked back toward the house.

Toward footsteps squishing through the grass and weeds all around them.

Chapter 10

Missy dropped one of Amy's hands and they turned to face what they couldn't see.

"I think we're out of time to keep the bad things inside," Amy said.

"Out of time to get over to my house and call for help, too."

Amy pointed a few yards off to their right, where a wide clump of vines with small, heart-shaped leaves made a huge flat spot in the rest of the tall weeds. Barefoot-shaped depressions crossed from one side to the other.

"Walking in circles again," Amy said, "same way they sounded in the house. If you have any ideas or guesses what this could possibly be or what we can do about it, I'd love to hear them right about now."

"My idea was to get out and come back with the police, remember?" Missy pointed to a shallow puddle on the other side of them, rippling as something unseen walked across it. "Or a preacher. They *are* circling, at least for now. You want me to guess, at least about one thing? I don't much like saying this or thinking on it, but I didn't see anything inside the house broken. Not even things that should have happened after thirty years, like stuff I see in old houses all the time. Did you?"

"Nothing besides the window we broke. And the lamp I dropped in the bedroom. Maybe we stirred them up by going inside?"

Missy took a step closer, and Amy let go of her hand and put an arm around her waist. She didn't mind one bit when Missy's arm went around her shoulders, warm and strong.

"We might have stirred them up, made them more active," Missy said. "But those footprints were everywhere when I first walked down that hallway. Maybe they kept the house from falling apart somehow, too."

"Wait, you said Great Auntie Maybelle talked about blocking the trapdoor to keep something from getting *out* through the floor. Not in. Maybe this started before she ever died."

Missy stared at Amy, brow furrowed, rainwater collecting in her fine black eyebrows.

"I said I couldn't remember what she said. But it could have been that. I always thought Maybelle imagined whatever it was 'cause of the way her mind was going at the end. Can't really say I think she imagined much of anything now."

Amy shook her head, trying to keep her overstrained mind from freezing up solid. The watery noises of things walking around them got louder with every passing minute. But no matter how closely she listened and watched, or how hard she concentrated, she didn't catch any of the ghostly impressions in the saturated ground getting closer.

Only circling, circling.

"I don't think I'll say anyone is imagining anything ever again," Amy said.

Thunder rumbled off in the distance, the same direction

the first storm came from. Amy felt Missy trembling against her, and wondered if Missy's heart beat as fast as her own.

"Much as I like standing here with you," Missy said, "we can't stand out in this rain forever. Couple steps toward the trail?"

Amy nodded, moving when Missy did.

The squishing, splashing noises got louder, and the marks in the weeds and mud between them and the house got closer.

The ones behind them, closer to the trail, stayed where they were.

Amy pulled them in the opposite direction, back toward the huge fallen tree and her trapped rental car.

Now the footsteps got faster and still closer between them and the house. Only a few feet away. And once again, the distance in the other three directions stayed the same.

"Maybe they…" Amy swallowed hard and raised her voice. "Are you wanting us to go back into the house?"

The steps slowed at once to their original pace, and Amy was certain the depressions in the matted weed retreated toward the house.

"If we go back inside," Missy said, "you'll keep out of the way and let us?"

This time the indentations moved all the way out of the flattened weeds.

Amy glanced toward the puddle behind them. "Closer all around us now except in one direction. I think our choice is made."

She dropped her arm and twined her fingers through Missy's, caught up in an aching wish that the two of them could get transported out of here somehow. To Missy's house or back into town at least, maybe all the way to her sad little temporary apartment in Chicago.

Anywhere without cold, pouring rain and another storm

coming and mysterious footprints and all this other nonsense.

Somewhere the two of them could think and talk and maybe figure out if they were holding onto each other out of fear and no other choice, or whether they fit together so nicely for a reason. If the closeness and fascination Amy remembered from all those years ago still existed.

Where they could *make* a choice, instead of trying to deal with choices being made for them.

"I don't much like it," Missy said. "But I think you're right. I might regret this, but I might not have the chance later on. Or the courage."

A flare of dancing, swirling heat in her chest gave Amy the slightest warning before Missy touched her cheek, leaned down, and set fire to her lips and heart and places she couldn't possibly focus on at that moment no matter how much she wanted to.

Chapter 11

BY THE TIME another fast-approaching thunderclap got her attention, Amy realized she was gripped tight in a full-on and altogether hot breast press with Missy, both of them breathing almost as hard as after sprinting up out of the basement.

And the footsteps around them had stopped.

"Do you hear…" Amy whispered against Missy's lips.

"Not a sound," Missy whispered back. "Not sure if that's good or bad."

"I'll tell you right now one thing that's good. Just in case I don't get the chance later." She kissed Missy hard and deep, groaning low in her throat before she let go and stepped back. "I hope we can figure out more if we get out of here."

Missy ducked her head low enough that she was looking up at Amy.

"*When* we get out of here, you're on."

They held hands and took a step toward the house, then another.

Their unseen escorts responded at once. This time the

noise and flattened spots stayed to the sides and behind them, leaving one clear path.

Right back to the cellar door at the back of the house.

"Guess we can't pretend they're not reacting to us," Amy said. "Or that they can't hear us or understand what we say."

"Nope. That would be fine and dandy if we had a clue what they want. Besides getting us back inside your house."

"And they still haven't hurt us. Not that I want to tempt fate and test that out."

The bottom step in front of the cellar door was invisible under several inches of mucky brown water, smelling like minerals and decaying forest. Amy retrieved the black metal drain cleaner from its hiding place in the stones and went to work, digging around at the sides.

As soon as she felt the forked metal end slip into and out of the drain, the water started sinking. Within a minute, the sodden bottom step still covered with moss and rotting leaves was visible.

So were the footprints passing by them, leaving muddy traces on the step and muddy prints on the wet concrete floor of the cellar. The oil lamp still burning showed each perfect bare foot shape appearing, moving across the floor and up the concrete steps into the house.

"Think we should try to touch them?" Amy whispered close to Missy's ear.

Missy shivered, then whispered back with her lips nearly against Amy's ear. Warm breath against cool skin made Amy shiver just as much.

"Maybe once we have a clear path to the door."

Amy couldn't exactly say she was comfortable back in the house. Somewhere past nervous and into afraid got close to the truth. But for some crazy reason, she wasn't anywhere near terrified like she had been before. Having the oil lamp back in her hand helped a little, sure.

But the air itself felt less ominous.

"What now?" Missy said, sounding more curious than afraid herself. "Back upstairs?"

"That's where everyone else seems to be going. At least we have a little bit more light."

The padlock under the trapdoor worked a lot easier this time, and they followed in the damp, muddy traces of whatever now seemed to be in charge of the whole operation.

Amy once again stood in the hallway, marveling at how many more footprints she saw on the dusty wooden floor, cutting darker paths through the thick dust. Whatever these ghosts or people or things were, there had to be dozens of them. All headed away from the pitch black hallway and back toward the kitchen.

The air even smelled fresher up here, more like rainstorm than musty closed-up house.

"Maybe they just want us to clean up the mess from breaking the window," Amy said.

"Maybelle would have liked that. Doesn't feel near as bad in here as it did before. Notice that?"

Amy nodded. "I still wouldn't volunteer to spend the night alone, but I'm not about to jump out of my skin this time."

Her mind volunteered the less than helpful suggestion that she might be feeling better simply because she didn't see Missy as a stranger or a potential enemy. Not anymore.

Perhaps not the best conclusion to reach after nothing more than a couple of (mind-blowing) kisses, but still true.

And still worth remembering to keep a damn close eye on her surroundings, which were probably no less threatening.

The invisible horde spaced itself out around them, so now the footprints and the odd thump-squeak noises moved in front, beside, and behind them. The varying cadences and patterns were back too, some toddler fast, some grownup slow.

The slow, ponderous gait with a dragged step in the middle finally resolved itself in Amy's reawakening memory.

"Does that sound like Great Auntie Maybelle's steps to you?" she said in a low voice, as if that could keep ghosts from overhearing. "That slower one?"

Missy blinked several times, and Amy realized she was fighting back tears.

"I think you're right. I remember her walking like that toward the end now that you say so. You don't think she's still here, do you? One of them?"

Amy laughed and squeezed Missy's hand.

"I didn't think one single thing about the last couple of days would be happening less than a week ago. So I'm probably the last person you should ask. But her being here all this time would explain why the inside is in such good shape. I kinda hope she's still here. As long as she's happy."

"Me too," Missy said.

The noise of the rain picking back up outside drowned out most of the footsteps once they reached the kitchen. The afternoon light was heavy and gray, leaving Amy thankful for the faint but warm illumination of the oil lamp.

Now that she was inside the kitchen—standing in front of the mist-covered cherry wood table instead of peering through the broken window—Amy recognized more of the results of all the trouble over the house.

And she saw more of what Missy meant by the house not looking like it had been abandoned for so terribly long.

Plenty of dust and loops of cobweb decorated the surfaces and the ceiling, but not one thing had been packed up or taken out of here, same as in the bedroom.

All of her Great Auntie Maybelle's fancy, flower-patterned dishes still sat in the glass-fronted display case. Her pots and pans, and a few cast-iron skillets handed down from ancestors Amy never met, still hung from the dark oak beams overhead.

Handmade and carefully maintained oval rag rugs in a dozen colors covered spots on the green and white linoleum. Plain blue and white everyday dishes waited in the drainer, and a cookbook with handwritten notes even sat open on the white tile counter.

A little girl inside of Amy fully expected her Great Auntie Maybelle to walk in with her slow, steady pace and start cooking prune cake from the recipe that must have been waiting for thirty years now.

The footsteps all around them stopped again.

"This is hard to take in," Amy said. "Except for the dust that she never would have allowed, it looks like she was standing here this morning."

Missy didn't bother wiping her tears.

"I never have seen a house that was empty for long look kept up like this one does. I always felt more at home over here than I ever did at my own house. Even scared half out of my wits, I still feel that way now."

"I think she kept a bunch of candles in one of those cabinets," Amy said. "We might need them if the storm gets as bad as it was before."

She started to turn away from the table and reach for the white cabinet doors, but her hand, arm, and shoulder plunged into what felt like a solid wall of clammy, almost fleshy versions of the cobwebs everywhere.

Amy wasn't the least bit ashamed of letting out a yelp. She dropped Missy's hand so she could try to rub the memory out of her flesh.

"What? Amy, what happened?"

"I think… I think I know what happens if we touch one of them. Can you try, see if it hits you the same way?"

Missy's brow wrinkled and her mouth turned down, but she thrust her hand out the same way Amy had. And yanked it back just as fast.

"That felt like *guts* or something. Cold, rotten *guts*."

"I got cobwebs, but the same general idea. They don't seem to want us to go wandering around right now."

Missy shrugged, rubbing at her hand.

"I guess that's fine for now, but I sure would like to know what they want us to do instead."

Amy froze at the squeak of a finger rubbing along wood.

"Did you…" Missy said, her voice no more than a breathy whisper.

"Look at the table."

Chapter 12

LINES CUT through the mist on the reddish wood without fingers or anything else to do the work. Different lines in more than one place, as if several of the ghosts started writing at once.

Amy grabbed Missy's hand again.

So glad both of you are finally here. House has been empty and lonely for too long. Missed my two favorite troublesome girls.

"My god, that's Maybelle," Missy said in a rough voice. "I can hear her saying those exact words plain as day."

"But how? Can we ask questions like we did outside? There seem to be all kinds of ghosts. Wait, I'm sorry, everyone who's here, does that word bother you? Ghosts?"

Unseen breath fogged the wood back up again before new words took shape. In the same neat, precise hand Amy remembered from countless letters and greeting cards.

I sure do hope all of us are long past caring about what the living call us. If ghosts *makes this easier on you, honey, you go right ahead. As to why we're here, that's right hard to say. Might be because of the way things turned bad for all of us who lived so long up here on this mountain.*

"Sounds to me like Julie must not be there," Missy said. "Not if you're talking that way."

Several seconds passed with no new words on the table. The only sound was a whispery shuffle, like all the feet around them shifted and moved. Amy jumped when the floor creaked under someone, and again when fresh writing appeared.

I'm real sorry Missy, nobody here has seen your mama. There's more places to go in between one life and the next than you'd believe until you get here yourself. To tell you the truth, none of us are supposed to be here, *wandering around in this old dusty house. Not for near this long. Should have moved on to somewhere else long and long ago. Either Julie already fetched up somewhere else like this, or she went on to her destination.*

Missy shook her head, wiping roughly at the tears on her face.

"Don't apologize on my account, ma'am. Or Julie's. If she's met her just reward somewhere she can't reach us, this world and the next are sure to be better places."

"If you're not supposed to be here," Amy said, "is there something we can do? I mean, I'm happy to have company if you let me walk around without blocking my way. Maybe stop trying to grab people with the closet curtains. And shoving your wardrobe off the trapdoor and dropping trees behind my car."

This time the table fogged over in a puffing pattern that Amy was certain came from laughter.

Lord, honey, I sure do wish we could do something like bring a tree down. I seem to recall someone in the rescue squad shoving my wardrobe over the day they rolled my body out of here. Today's the first any of us got outside the walls or even down into that cellar 'cause we couldn't even get the blasted trapdoor open.

Now as far as that curtain, a couple of the young'uns figured out how to puff it out that way, managed to sneak away and do it. Clever as they are, they know what they got to do now.

The fog returned and waited undisturbed long enough for Amy to glance up at Missy, eyebrows raised.

Then much smaller lines appeared, but not with words at first. A circle with dots for eyes and a frowning mouth showed up. Then ragged writing, nothing like Great Auntie Maybelle's hand.

Sorry we scared you.

"Well, thank you," Missy said with a half smile. "Guess you had to get our attention somehow. I got no reason to doubt we're talking to Maybelle Johnstone. But who else is here? Sounded like dozens of people walking before."

This time the pause was long enough that both Amy and Missy carefully pulled chairs away from the table, making sure they didn't bump into the clammy remnants of the ghosts behind them. About the time they sat, marks started upon the table.

This here is everyone in both our families that already passed on from years and years ago. Farther back than even this house has stood. Johnstones and Phillips both. They started showing up a few at a time, round the time I started to get so run down and sick. After the trouble started between us. Thought I was confused at first, or more confused than I had been.

But they made powerful company for lonely nights. That's why I didn't want them to go. Probably could have continued on their way if I hadn't trapped them all up here with me, but I appreciate them staying just the same.

"You *did* say keeping them from getting out," Amy said. "And then we went and let them out through this window. I'm sorry, Great Auntie Maybelle."

No, honey, don't you dare apologize. I figure we've all been here waiting long enough. Maybe it finally is time for us to move on and let the living get on with their lives. And let the living take care of this house and put an end to all this bad blood that never should have been here in the first place.

"You mean us?" Missy said, watching Amy. "I get the feeling Amy wants to head back to the big city first chance she gets, but you know I'll do whatever I can."

Amy opened her mouth, meaning to make some kind of protest, but she hoped for the distraction of words squeaking their way across the table instead.

She tried to keep her relief to herself when the words started.

Now is that what either one of you wants? If you do, we'll all work things out as best we can. But I lived longer than both of you put together and then some, and made more than my fair share of mistakes. I know what I mean when I say you'd do best to think on what you really want *while you got the chance.*

These kinds of things are best left private between two people, I know that. But I got to say I remember how you both lit up at the sight of each other all those years ago. The way you're sparking to each other now makes it plain as day that the draw is still right there between you.

Amy stared into Missy's dark blue eyes, knowing she couldn't possibly make up her mind about one single thing right now.

Not about keeping or selling the house. Not about her miserably disrupted life back in Chicago.

Not even about the woman sitting beside her. Her long-ago and nearly forgotten little-girl friend. The grown woman who'd managed in a handful of hours to make some of the mess and noise inside of Amy feel calm and happy again even though she'd spent most of it scared to death, when she wasn't sure calm and happy would ever happen.

"I don't know what I want to do," Amy said. "Not yet. But I know it's been way too long since I spent some time here. And that I've spent enough years reacting to everything around me. My life in general is up in the air enough that I'm ready to take some time and *think* about what I want to do next." She touched Missy's cheek, then brushed her hand along her shoulder and arm until their fingers linked together. "I hope you are, too."

Missy held her expression too carefully neutral, especially with the way her lovely full lips tried not to twitch into a smile.

"Well, I did promise Art Steffens I'd help you get this place straightened up. If we both find a few more areas in our lives that could stand some repairs and attention, might be good to work on those, too."

Amy laughed, brushing away happy tears of her own.

"Will you be here, Great Auntie Maybelle? At least for a little while? I'm pretty sure we could use the help."

That puffing mist covered the table again.

Ghost laughter.

I reckon I could stay for a while, see to it that things get put right. Much as I can, anyway. I might like to do some traveling of my own, but I got to admit I'm curious how this old place will turn out with new life in it.

"New life," Missy said. "I sure do like the sound of that."

Amy leaned over and kissed her, a shy, almost chaste kiss with who knew how many members of both their families watching. Joy rocketed through her just the same.

She kept her thoughts to herself, but she had no doubt Missy understood.

Maybe new love, too.

Chapter 13

Amy sat on the new porch swing in front of her old house, watching the sun set over the mountains in unusually warm October air. Her work laptop perched on the special swing desk Missy had rigged up for her. All so Amy could spend as much time outside as possible while the weather lasted. And so she could kick herself into motion any time she wanted to.

She still caught a faint scent of pine from the swing and the new boards of the rebuilt porch itself. Three months of hard work—and the maintenance account her Great Auntie Maybelle set up long ago—had almost everything put to right.

Even the honeybees were settled into their new home a couple of miles away and getting ready for the winter. A couple of jars of honey extracted from the house's wall still waited in the kitchen for tea or cooking.

Amy barely jumped when Missy spoke from right behind her. She'd heard Missy's truck coming along the driveway about fifteen minutes ago, but she'd never quite worked out the trick of hearing Missy herself approaching.

Somehow Missy managed to move more quietly than a ghost.

"About ready to knock off for the night?" Missy said.

"All finished. What time will Art and his friends get here for dinner?"

Missy walked around and sat close beside Amy, all flannel shirt and blue jeans and sawdust and sexy clean sweat.

"About an hour. Whatever you've got going on in the kitchen smells amazing."

Amy scooted closer so she could rest her head against Missy's strong shoulder.

"That's the prune cake. I've just about got Great Auntie Maybelle's recipe down, once I talked her into giving me a few tips she never *wrote* down. Took me long enough."

Missy kissed the top of Amy's head. "You keep on practicing, and I'll keep on eating up the results."

"You said you know the people Art's bringing for dinner? Someone from town?"

"Don't know them too well, no. That's the house I've been working on this week. Nice couple. Beth, the one who owns it, wants to make sure there's enough storage for two. Seems her new fiancé Mark just moved in over the summer. He thinks there's plenty of room, of course. She figures there's never enough room, and that more shelves than they could ever fill are cheap insurance for a happy marriage."

Missy laughed out loud, the sweet songbird sound warming Amy's whole body.

"They'll be able to fill us in on their side of exactly why the town changed from Hartstown to Bountyfield, too. Beth refused to say anything until she can talk to both of us."

Amy laughed in return and nodded. "Smart woman. Looking forward to meeting them."

Since the day they'd first gotten inside and talked to Great Auntie Maybelle, Missy and a couple of her construction buddies had transformed the house. Besides the new porch, they'd remodeled the Seventies bathroom, painted all the other rooms, built a proper walk-in closet that went all the way to the ceiling, and made sure honeybees couldn't move into the stone walls again.

Amy and Missy were careful to keep the polished cherry wood breakfast table Amy's Great Uncle Harmon made in exactly the same spot under the repaired kitchen window, and kept it clear in case any of their ghostly houseguests wanted to talk.

Missy made a gorgeous oak dining room table for them to use instead, with wood from the tree that fell across the road and kept them from running away the day of the big storm. Since that tree kept both of them from running away from each other, Missy used the rest of the wood in repairs all over the house.

Great Auntie Maybelle had taken her own advice and decided to do a bit of traveling around the next worlds. She refused to tell Amy or Missy much about it when she stopped by, insisting they needed to learn such things on their own when the time came.

The other family ghosts dropped in from time to time when they needed a break from their own travels. And they were every bit as stubborn about sharing their adventures with the living.

Everyone was too happy about the visits to ask too many questions, except when it came to Amy wanting to get those recipes just right.

Amy and Missy had left the trap door open at night for a few weeks, too, until all the ghosts admitted they'd satisfied their curiosity about the one place they couldn't walk to for so many years. Now they got their walking in during the day so the living could sleep at night.

As far as weekday pursuits, Missy set the whole place up

with Wi-Fi once she realized they could tap into the light-ning-fast fiber optic line running across the mountain and down into Bountyfield. Something about Amy being able to do her remote work out on the porch, or inside by the huge picture window in bad weather, more than made up for having a bunch of noisy coworkers back in Chicago.

Waking up beside Missy under her great-aunt's crazy quilt every morning surely had an awful lot to do with Amy feeling a whole lot less lonely, too.

"I guess we better get ready," Missy said, though she put her arm around Amy and seemed to settle in rather than moving. "I get the feeling Beth and Mark are looking forward to talking to us about what all happened up here. You know, when you first got here."

"You *told* them about that?"

Amy hadn't breathed a word to anyone. She suspected Art Steffens knew more than he was letting on, but he'd never admitted it. Tonight might be a perfect time to bring that up.

Missy kicked the porch swing into motion.

"I didn't say a word. Beth seems to have an idea about such things, almost like the second sight that the old folks used to talk about. You know, those silly old wives tales neither of us believe in."

Amy sat up long enough to plant a long, welcome-home kiss on Missy, with a promise of more to come once *all* the company left them alone for the night.

"Oh yeah," she said. "All that old wives nonsense. Like ghosts and haunted houses."

Missy winked. "And childhood friends turning into sweethearts thirty years down the road."

Amy smiled and leaned in for another kiss.

"Exactly like that."

ABOUT KARI

The daughter, granddaughter, and great-granddaughter of coal miners, Kari Kilgore's wanderlust and imagination lead her all over the world on grand adventures. Her heart and family bring her home to her native Appalachian Mountains of Virginia. From that solid base, she and her husband Jason A. Adams bring those adventures to life in fiction.

Kari writes science fiction, fantasy, and horror, and she's happiest when she surprises herself. She lives at the end of a long dirt road in the middle of the woods with Jason, various house critters, and wildlife they're better off not knowing more about.

The Confidential Adventure Club

For Kari's exclusive free After The End stories and deleted scenes, discounts, early pre-sale releases, adorable pet photos, and a whole lot more not available anywhere else, check out The Confidential Adventure Club at www.smarturl.it/c-a-club.

Hope to see you there!

www.karikilgore.com
www.spiralpublishing.net

ALSO BY KARI KILGORE

I hope you enjoyed *Walking the Ghosts* as much as I enjoyed writing it. If you're curious about Beth, Mark, and Art, the three joining Amy and Missy for dinner at the end, check out *Songs in the Mountain*. That's the story of how Mark and Beth met. Next is *Secrets in the Land*—Mark's return for a new adventure with Beth, right before Amy and Missy meet up. Both of those and much more are available at www.karikilgore.com.

The Confidential Adventure Club

Want more fiction from Kari, including stories, discounts, and box sets not available anywhere else? Want to hear about locations, research, and other cool things that inspired this story and beyond? All that and adorable pet photos, too?

Join The Confidential Adventure Club and get a thank you gift of a free short story and a whole lot more at www.smarturl.it/c-a-club.

Hope to see you there!

The Storms of Future Past Series:

Dreaming the Storm

Joining the Storm

Into the Storm

Fighting the Storm

Sensing the Storm: A Storms of Future Past Prequel Story

Storms of Future Past Books One through Four Collection

The Voices through Time Series:

Songs in the Mountain

Secrets in the Land

Walking the Ghosts: A Voices through Time Novella

Dispatches from the Galaxy Stories:

Restricted Species

The Becalmed

The Garbage Belt

Terminalia Short Stories:

Terminalia

Little Five

Novels:

Until Death

The Dream Thief

Novellas:

Legacy of the Land

In the Pines

Collections:

Fantastic Women: A Dark Fantasy Novella Trio

Fantastic Shorts: Volume 1 - A Fantasy Short Story Collection

Near Future Forward (with Jason A. Adams)

Short Stories:

Intentions, The Seeds of Love, Wicked Bone, The Sound of Murder, Reflections, The Last Dragonkeeper, The Earworms

"Kari Kilgore is an author to watch—her lyrical voice a siren song; her insight, conjured voodoo."

—Richard Thomas, author of *Breaker* and *Tribulations*